A REAL FAIRY TALE

WRITTEN BY ISABELLA ZUZULA AND GRANDMOMMY

ILLUSTRATED BY SHAY DEES

COVER BY DAVE JORDAN

A FAIRY TALE
Copyright 2020 by Isabella Zuzula

ISBN: 9798692096845
First Edition: October 2020

CONTENTS

FOREWORD

Over the Christmas Break in 2019, my five grandchildren were visiting me in Florida. My oldest grandson, Calvin, and my only granddaughter, Isabella, were talking about what their New Year's resolutions were going to be for the year 2020. They both made a resolution to write a book and try to get it published.

In March 2020, the whole country went into quarantine because of the COVID-19 virus.

I thought that this would be a good time for Isabella to write the book that she had indicated was her goal for the year (Calvin is still looking for his topic). I wanted to do it with her so we could spend the time together even though we couldn't be together in person. We both thought that writing would make the quarantine go much faster!

We hope you enjoy our story!

1
TH START OF AN AMAZING STORY

My name is Isabella and I am 10 years old. I have an absolutely amazing story to tell you but it's not really my story. It's my Grandmommy's story but, maybe, it's not her story either. It's really the Fairies' story and, yes, Fairies are real. I know that because they have been my friends for seven years.

This story starts seven years ago. My Grandmommy bought five fairy houses and three fairy statues because she thought my cousins and I would like them. Oh, I should tell you that my Grandmommy and Papa have five grandchildren. Calvin is 13, Robby is 12, Graham is 11, I'm 10 and Henry is 9. Yep, I'm the only girl and I could write stories and stories about THAT but this is the Fairies' story.

Grandmommy made a Fairy garden under the trees up north. We live in Michigan and we spend a great deal of the summer up north on a lake. I can write stories and stories about the fun we have at the lake but, again, that is another story! Now this becomes my Grandmommy's story so she needs to write the next part.

Ok, I'm Isabella's Grandmommy. I did find these really cute fairy houses in a catalog and I thought they would be a great addition to my garden. Fairy statues were also offered in the catalog so I ordered some of both. I made a great garden for them and I couldn't wait for my grandkids to see it! However, I had no idea that a small garden was going to change my life and my grandchildren's lives forever.

2
DISCOVERING THE FAIRIES

One night, I was sitting on my deck looking at the houses that I had set out for the fairies and I saw these little tiny lights around the garden. I thought they were fireflies. We have so many of them in Michigan! But now I know, maybe they weren't all fireflies. I had three little fairy statues in my fairy garden and they all seemed to light up at the same time. Then, the statues went dark. I thought it was rather strange but I didn't realize that a wonderful miracle had just occurred.

The next morning, I went outside and walked over to my fairy garden. All my fairy statues had moved. They hadn't moved far but I was really, really sure they had moved. I stood there and looked and looked at them. They were all standing up so I knew that the wind hadn't moved my fairy statues. I didn't have the slightest idea how they could have moved.

For some unknown reason, I sat down and started to talk to these little statues. I told them that I had five incredibly special grandchildren that I didn't get to see as much as I wanted to see them and I really missed them all the time. I had bought three statues and they were all boy fairies so I told them that I was going to buy one girl fairy and one more boy fairy. I wanted each of my four grandsons to have a boy fairy statue and my only granddaughter to have a girl fairy statue.

I bought the two additional fairies and put them in my garden. That night, I sat on my deck after it was dark and I was looking in the direction of my fairy garden. At around midnight, I saw five fireflies light up my fairy statues and go up into the sky! They seemed to be dancing and chasing each other.

I stayed as quiet as I could and just watched for hours. The fireflies never went far from the Fairy Garden and then, when the sky started to get light from the rising sun, they all landed back on the little statues and seemed to disappear.

The next day, I walked out to my garden and all five statues had moved. Yes, they had moved again. I really didn't know why or how they were moving. It made absolutely no sense to me. You see, it never, ever crossed my mind that fairies were real. Obviously, I had a mystery on my hands and I was determined to solve it!

I asked my friends who had Fairy Gardens if they had ever noticed fireflies around their gardens. They all said that they hadn't noticed any flies. This mystery was even more puzzling. I simply could not figure out why fireflies seemed to like my fairy statues.

Since I was still working on my Fairy Garden to make it incredibly special, I continued talking to my little fairy statues as I worked. I told them stories about my grandchildren and how much they were going to love this garden. For three days, I worked in the garden and, every night, I watched the fireflies leave my statues to dance and play.

I bought five more statues (all girls) to put in the Fairy Garden and then waited that night to see what would happen. You guessed it. Five MORE fireflies came into the garden and danced with the other five fireflies that night. When daylight came, all ten of them landed on the fairy statues and went dark.

I was stunned and I realized that something wonderful and miraculous was happening in my Fairy Garden. They were not fireflies. Fairies were REAL and, for some reason, they had picked my garden to live!

3
TALKING TO FAIRIES

I was so excited that I couldn't sleep. I couldn't wait to go out to my Fairy Garden and try to talk to these little Fairies. I really didn't know how to talk to Fairies. Actually, I never even thought that fairies were real so, of course, I never thought about talking to them. Think about it. How would YOU talk to a fairy? Do they understand English or do Fairies have their own language? I certainly didn't know the answers to these questions and, since no one believed Fairies were real, I couldn't find the answers on the internet. I was going to have to figure this out on my own and, maybe, with help from my grandchildren.

I decided to do what I had been doing for days. I sat down and just talked to them. I told them that I was speaking words that humans call 'English', I told them more stories about my grandchildren and that humans have 'adults' and 'children' and adults have lived more years.

I first told them that adults were big humans and children were little humans. Then, I realized that this would confuse them because I'm a little adult and my children are way bigger than me. I also knew that my grandchildren would probably be taller than me some day. I talked and I talked and I talked. I talked about all and everything that came into my mind.

During the day, the Fairies never moved. Not a single inch. They never even twitched or wriggled. So, I would watch them at night and they would always fly out of their earthly statue and dance and play. I wanted to communicate with them SO much but my talking didn't seem to be working at all.

Finally, one morning I walked out to the Garden with my cup of tea and sat down to talk to them. I was chattering away and then I noticed a piece of paper under a rock by one of the houses. I reached down and picked the note up, wondering how the paper ended up under a rock. It was folded in half so I unfolded it and read this message, "Do little humans like to play?"

My legs went completely weak and I sat down hard. I read the message over and over and stared at my Fairies. I finally whispered, "Is this a message from you? Are you trying to talk to me?" Of course, they didn't answer but I sat there with my mouth wide open and my eyes the size of the moon. Were my Fairies actually WRITING to me? Could this even be possible?

That night, I sat on the deck watching them play and I wondered many things. Has any human ever communicated with a Fairy before me or was I just imaging things? I couldn't think of another explanation for that note but how was it possible for Fairies to write me a note? That didn't make any sense at all. I went to bed but, again, I couldn't sleep. I felt like I was starting the most amazing adventure that a human had ever experienced.

4
THE FAIRIES WANT TO PLAY

I was actually afraid to go out to the Garden the next morning. I was afraid I had imagined the whole thing. However, when I arrived, there was another note under the same rock. My hands were shaking so badly that I could barely open the folded note. I took a deep breath and read it. It said, "Yes. We want to know if your little humans would play with us."

I felt water running down my cheeks and I realized that I was crying for joy. These most wonderful Fairies wanted to play with my Grandchildren! A week ago, I never imagined Fairies were real and now we were talking to each other! Well, I was talking and they were writing but that's still communication!

Finally, I was able to calm myself and I told them my grandchildren would love to play with them but human children slept at night and played during the day. I also told them that my grandchildren were very little in human years and they might not be as careful as they needed to be with the Fairies being so fragile. I didn't know how my grandchildren were going to be able to play with the Fairies and, if they couldn't see the Fairies at night, how were they going to know they were real?

I then asked the Fairies why I was the only adult human that knew they were real. I asked them to leave me another note because it didn't seem that they could talk. I couldn't understand why they could write messages in English but not talk at all. There was so much about Fairies that I didn't know at all!

The next morning, I ran out of my house to see if the Fairies had left me a note. I was fairly sure they had done so because they seemed to want to talk to me as much as I wanted to talk to them. I was right. The folded note was under the same rock as the past two days.

It read as follows, "A human needs magic to see and talk to Fairies. We are magical creatures. You have magic. You see us. Maybe little humans will have magic. We want see these little humans so we can play."

I could tell that English wasn't their normal language but I was amazed how well they seemed to know it. I wished that I knew fairy language but I didn't even know that they were real until a few days ago.

I could not wait for my grandchildren to meet the Fairies for the first time! Do my grandchildren have the necessary magic to see them? Would they love them as much as I already did?

5
THE FIRST SUMMER

This is Isabella writing again. I was really young when I first met the Fairies. When Grandmommy first showed me the fairy garden, I was amazed the fairies had chosen to live in my Grandmommy's garden! I was little but I knew these fairies were going to be part of my life for an exceptionally long time.

I remember how much I adored their colorful houses and outfits. I loved their tiny little wings and how detailed they were in their faces. To me, these fairies were the most wonderful, extraordinary things I had ever seen! The fact that they moved around every night and left us notes was just remarkable!

I remember that every time I arrived at the lake house, I would sprint down the long sidewalk and into the front yard. I couldn't wait to see my fairy friends and their Garden! Then, I would sit down and talk to the fairies and tell them about what I had been doing since I last saw them.

I loved the Fairy Garden so I protected it from my rough brother and cousins. I couldn't touch the fairies because Grandmommy told me that their wings were too fragile. Remember, I was only 3 years old when I first met them. All I could do was yell at the boys and say, "Don't touch the Fairies! Don't touch the Fairies!" All that yelling worked! From then on, I made sure that the boys were always careful around the Garden. Even though I was one of the youngest, I felt very responsible towards the fairies and I wanted to keep them safe.

Grandmommy told me and my cousins that we could actually touch the fairies when we were older. I had such a hard time waiting to be 'older'!

The first summer was so much fun for me sharing the Fairies with my grandchildren. Isabella, Calvin, Robby, Graham and Henry mostly sat on the grass and talked to the Fairies in the Fairy Garden because they knew that they weren't allowed to touch them. I explained to them that fairy wings were very fragile so it would be best if we never touched them. Every morning, the Fairies were in a different place, though, so they loved finding where the Fairies had moved.

My grandchildren loved their new Fairy friends! From the first time they saw them, they knew they were real and acted as if they were simply new friends. As the Fairies said, I am an adult that still believes in magic and I was so happy that all my grandchildren seemed to inherit that gift from me. Isabella did love them the most but the boys enjoyed talking to them and writing notes to them also.

Isabella did ask me why they could never see the Fairies fly and I explained to them that they only would fly at night when it was very dark. I didn't know why they only flew at night and I never thought to ask them for years. When I finally did ask them years later, I was very surprised at their answer! However, that answer will have to wait to be told much later in this book.

The summer went too quickly and soon was coming to an end. On the last weekend of the summer, the grandchildren went over to the Fairy Garden and said goodbye to their new friends and told the fairies that they would see them next summer. I was going to spend the Fall at the lake house so I promised my grandchildren that I would take care of our Fairies. One day, I was out in the yard and I could not find any of the Fairies in the Garden. The weather was getting cold and I was rather worried about them. I looked for them every day for a week but they were gone.

You have no idea how sad I was. We all loved the Fairies so much and we knew how lucky we were that they had chosen OUR Garden to live. I worried all winter that I would never see them again so it was a sad winter. I shouldn't have worried, though. It turns out the Fairies love us as much as we love them!

6
HERE WE GO AGAIN!

Every May, I would take all the Fairy houses and accessories out of storage and build the Fairy Garden. I did it by myself the first years because Isabella was too young to help. Isabella and her brother Robby live in Michigan so, when they were older, they would come up to the Lake House in May and help me set up the Garden. It has become so big that Robby said this year, "Grandmommy, by the time I'm 30, this Garden will be the size of the entire yard!"
It IS big and it sure is nice that Isabella and Robby are old enough to help me now.

I had picked a nice spot between two big trees that had plenty of room to grow the Garden every year. The houses were of all colors, shapes, and sizes. I would use pretty blue stones to make a stream and a pond and I put bridges over the stream and little ducks in the pond. I planted little flowers and bought a little swing and seesaw so the Fairies would have a fun playground. Plenty of little benches were scattered around so the Fairies could sit during the day if they desired. They would need to pick a bench before they settled down for the day because, remember, Fairies can only move at night.

It always took me a few days to complete the Garden and I always hoped that the Fairies would come back. I never knew if they would return and it made me so sad just thinking that we may not see them. Because of that, I tried to make our Fairy Garden the very best Garden in the world. I didn't want them to decide to live somewhere else!

On Memorial Day, the Fairies have always returned!!! We would wait for them all day long and, sometimes, we would get nervous because we would not see them. However, when we would wake up the next day, the Fairies had arrived and had made themselves right at home again in the Garden as if they had never left. From then on, we always knew it was going to be a GREAT summer!

Every year, I make the Fairy Garden bigger and bigger and more fairies come to stay with us. By the time Isabella was seven years old, the Fairy

Garden was really a Fairy Village! I had added a beach with beach chairs, beach blankets, and a Tiki Hut. I always tried to think of things that would make the Fairies happy.

The first few years, my grandchildren were too little to do much except talk to the Fairies but it sure became a lot more fun when Isabella was about seven years old. The Fairies were very, very curious about human children. My grandchildren had always been very gentle with them so they were starting to trust little humans more and more. The Fairies had so many questions and Isabella was old enough to start trying to answer their questions every day.

7
MORE FUN FOR THE FAIRIES

Grandmommy told you how she added houses and playgrounds to the Fairy Garden every year. When I was seven, Grandmommy told me that I was old enough to help plan the new additions to the Garden. Grandmommy was doing a really good job but she's an adult and she needed me to think like the fairies. I looked at the pictures of the Garden from the year before and decided that the fairies would really love a cozy campsite and a colorful carnival.

For the campsite, we added tents, campers, and bonfires. We added a Ferris wheel, and some little food stations to the Carnival. Oh, we also added a really neat train and a Merry Go Round. The fairies always love the new additions that we added to the Garden and, due to how big the fairy garden is now, there are tons of fairies. Each year, more and more fairies arrive to live in the Garden.

Grandmommy just read my paragraph and she told me to pick the next addition. I think this year, we should plan to add on to the playground. The playground that we have now already has a slide, see-saw, and some fun flower seats. I'm going to add some hoops that the fairies can fly through and some monkey bars. Also, I'm planning to paint the monkey bars baby blue with either pink swirls or green swirls.

The fairies are going to be buff and that may be either a good or bad thing!

8
ISABELLA TRIES TO EXPLAIN

My cousins and I are always up to something at the Lake! We are busy all day floating on inner tubes, swimming, boating, playing yard games, having carnivals with our cousins and playing sports together. Whenever we are finished with an activity, the fairies would have so many questions. They wanted to know what we were playing or, if we went out on the lake in the inner tubes, they would leave us a note the next day saying, "Those floatable benches are really funny!"

I was on a paddle board one day with my Aunt Dana and the fairies wanted to know why I was walking on water. Since I never get their notes until the next day, it took me awhile to figure out that they didn't see the paddle board so they thought I was strolling on the water with my Aunt! The fairies always keep things interesting in a fun way!

You probably know that fairies don't grow bigger in size, only in knowledge. So, when my cousins and I went up to the Lake every year, they would always wonder, "How do these little humans keep on getting bigger and bigger every year?" My Grandmommy and I had to explain that human children grow bigger until they are adults. Though, sometimes it's a challenge when you try to explain things to fairies. This is because fairies don't really know the definition of things or how to use things. So, we must try and explain everything in the Fairy way and it's always a fun challenge!

Having the fairies around is an amazing experience that I'm honored to have in my life!

As Isabella said, explaining why the children were getting bigger to the Fairies was extremely hard. Fairies always stay the same size and, I guess, they stay the same age. The first few summers, they thought that different little humans were coming to play with them. Every summer, they seemed to be very shy again and I would ask them why they didn't remember Calvin, Robby, Graham, Isabella and Henry. I always received the same note under the rock the next morning, "New little humans we don't know. They hurt us?"

I would always answer, "No, these are the same children from last summer." It took me three years to realize that the Fairies never changed so they didn't know that human children grew and changed as they became older.

Isabella and I decided that we should probably try to explain why she looked different every year to the Fairies. We knew that we could just stand by the Garden and talk to them and, if they had more questions, they would write them on the note for the following morning (I guess they did their writing at night!). We told them that every year, human children have a birthday and they are one year older in age. Well, their next note said, "What is birthday and year? What is age?"

Isabella and I looked at each other and said, "This is sure going to be difficult to explain." First, we had to think of a way to explain a 'year' to them. We talked about it and decided, maybe, we could explain 'year' by telling them that every time they left when the air turned cold and came back to the Fairy Village when the air was warm was a year.

They replied, "Now know year. What is birthday and age?"

THAT was even harder to explain because we didn't know if Fairies were actually born. It is very hard to try to think like a Fairy when we are learning about them at the same time! So, we decided just to tell them that every human child has one special day a year that is the day that they are one year older. We thought we had explained it VERY well but they replied with this note the next day, "What is day and what is older?"

Isabella told you that sometimes it was hard to explain things to the Fairies! Explaining a day was easy, we just told them that a day was the time they stayed in the garden and one time of playing in the dark. We gave up trying to explain 'older'. We just said that older meant human children get taller on that day.

The next day, the note from the Fairies read, "Now we know same children all the years!" The Fairies were happy that they now understood!

9
COUSINS' WEEK

Every year around the 4th of July weekend, all my cousins on my Mom's side of the family would either drive or fly here to Higgins Lake, Michigan. We always play games such as corn hole, giant connect four, bucket toss, ring toss, obstacle races, kayak races and long jumping contests.

For the past two years, when Cousins' Week arrived, we would call ourselves future Olympians. We play the games, as I mentioned above, and Grandmommy kept score on who won. After five days of games, we would have a medal ceremony. The ceremony includes giving out bronze, silver and gold medals and Amazon gift cards to the three cousins who had the three highest scores in each event. I've always won the kayak race, even though I'm the second to the youngest out of nine cousins. Size and age don't matter if you try harder than anyone else!

The medal that I always work for the hardest, though, is the Sportsmanship award. Sometimes, it's hard to congratulate your cousin when he just beat you at a game but that's what good Sportsmanship is all about. I've always been in the medal round for the Sportsmanship award and I'm very proud of that accomplishment!

Higgins Lake Olympics is one of the highlights of the year (in my opinion).

When we had Cousins' Week for the first time, the fairies met four more human children who are my cousins. I thought the fairies would be nervous but they loosened up quicker than I thought that they would. My cousins loved the fairies. My cousin Kate (the only girl cousin besides me) seemed to pay attention to the fairies a little more than the boys did. That's actually normal because girls seem to have a little more magic than boys do.

However, all the cousins loved the fairies. They weren't really amazed until Grandmommy and I told them the fairies' story. Then, they were pretty amazed about how the fairies came to us instead of anybody else in the whole Universe!

The fairies love watching us play our Junior Olympic Games. We play the yard games right in front of them and, if they pick the right spot to stand or sit, they can also watch the long jump and kayak races. I noticed that throughout Cousins' week, the entire Village of fairies crowd onto their beach, the campsites, or the first row of houses because those are the best views of the games.

I would always remind my cousins (Dominic, Kate, Calvin, Brennan, Graham, Ryan and Henry) that they couldn't touch the fairies and they listened. Even though I was the second youngest, whenever it came to the fairies, I had the fairies' backs no matter how small I was individually.

10
WHERE DO HUMAN CHILDREN GO?

The fairies always would wonder why the children left the Lake house when summer was over. They didn't know that what humans call 'summer' was over but I didn't want to try to explain all the seasons to them! I had such a hard time explaining birthdays to them so I sure didn't want to try to explain how our 'year' was divided into four seasons. Whew. They just knew that we would play with them for months and then we were gone.

The fairies were always very sad after the children said goodbye so Grandmommy would spend extra time with them. I know that helped them but I think fairies are children and they really missed watching the human children play.

I thought I would try to explain to them that children need to go to school when the air starts to get cooler. I told them that we go to school to learn, to play sports and to see our friends. I told them that I have fairy friends and I also have human children friends.

I knew I was going to have to explain sports to them so I said that sports consist of a group of children that play a game together. I play a game that I kick a ball into a net. That game is called 'soccer'. I also play basketball but I didn't want the fairies to be confused over kicking the ball or dribbling the ball!

Some of that explanation made no sense to them. The next morning, they wrote and asked us what 'school' was and what was 'learn'. My Grandmommy and I went over to the fairies and explained to them about school. I told them that school was a building where all the children sat at desks or on the floor and the teacher tells us about new things. A teacher is someone like me (Isabella) who explains things to children just like I explain things to fairies like you.

The fairies wrote a note to us the next morning and it read, "Why do human children have to sit in a box all day?" I have NO idea why they thought we sit in a box! Sometimes it's really hard not to laugh when I read their notes but I don't want the fairies to think that I'm laughing at them. We, once again, needed to explain that we didn't have to sit down all day, a building wasn't a box and we left school every day to come back to our house every night. Though the fairies were still a little confused, they seemed to understand that we had to leave when the air was cooler because human children had different lives than fairies.

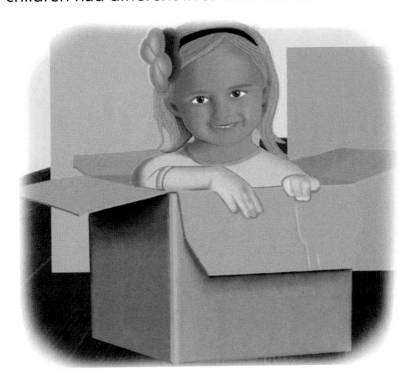

11
THE BIG STORM

One day, we rode our boats out to a beach across the lake and the wind started to pick up. My Papa looked at the weather forecast and realized that there were storms coming our way, so we decided to pack up all the food, towels and water toys quickly. We all jumped on the boats and went high-speed on the way back to the Lake House.

When we got back, I could barely see because of the high wind speed and all my hair whipping across my face. I had a lot of towels and my backpack in my hands. I made sure to hold on to them tightly so they wouldn't blow away. When I was running down the dock, I noticed our swimming platform's ladder was down in the water. I quickly put everything down on the dock, jumped in the water, and put the ladder up on platform so it wouldn't break off in the waves. The waves were already much bigger than normal because of the wind.

I grabbed everything again and ran down the dock, up onto the patio and into the house. I quickly dropped the towels and backpack on the floor and ran back outside to help prepare for the storm. My Grandmommy and my brother Robby were grabbing all the chair cushions so they wouldn't blow away in the wind. I ran down to the beach to help my Papa put all the kayaks onto their racks and grabbed any other loose items that I could find to bring into the house.

When we had everything that could blow away in the house, my Grandmommy told my brother and I to go downstairs where there weren't any windows. She told us a flat tornado was upon us. I went downstairs but then, realized that we forgot something.

"Grandmommy, Grandmommy!" I yelled with fear. "We forgot to bring the fairies into the house. They're going to get hurt!"

"Don't worry," my Grandmommy told me. "Trust me, they will be fine. They'll go into their houses and come back out when the storm is over."

"Okay," I replied, feeling relieved.

Finally, when the storm was over, I ran outside and saw that our neighbor's tree had fallen over, another neighbor's boat had torn away from the dock and was sitting on the beach, somebody's dock was broken and a couple of fairies had fallen over.

My Grandmommy had been right. Overall, the fairies were okay, just a little frightened. Apparently, two of the fairies (twins) named Lightening and Thunder really enjoyed the storm and had been flying in it. Those are two crazy fairies! The experience was pretty scary but the fairies were fine.

The Fairy Garden was a mess, though, so my brother and I had to get it cleaned up. A big branch had fallen but, luckily, it missed the Village by a few inches. We had to clean out leaves, little branches and a ton of acorns while being careful not to disturb the fairies or frighten them. It took us quite a while to finish it but our fairies are worth as much time as needed!

12
NAMING THE FAIRIES

Isabella mentioned in the last chapter that the Fairies have names. You are probably wondering how in the world did we know the names of our Fairy friends. Well, I can tell you, it wasn't easy.

We should have mentioned by now that the Fairies were ALWAYS listening to us. When Isabella and I (and the boys Calvin, Robby, Graham and Henry) would be talking by the Fairy Garden, we would always call each other by our names.

One day, I found a note under the note rock and it read, "You Grandmommy? Isabella little human child with long hair? Calvin, Robby, Graham, Henry little many human child with short hair?"

After all these years with the Fairies, I knew immediately what they were asking and I was thrilled! They knew our names! They also realized that each human had a different name. I asked them if they had names and waited for the note to be under the rock the next morning.

The next few days were a bit frustrating. They had replied that they did have what they called 'fairy calling' but I could not figure out the words they were writing. Since their note was full of names like 'hdhd', 'mwer' and 'wwwins', I decided that they must be writing in fairy language and I didn't know a word of fairy.

I told them that I didn't understand so I thought I should try an experiment. One night before I went to bed, I told them that I was going to leave a piece of white paper on the deck. I asked them if they could draw pictures to help me or leave something on the paper as a clue about their names.

When I woke up the next day, the paper had several items on it. There was an acorn, a bird feather, a flower, a blueberry (I had NO idea where they found that!) and a ladybug (I also had NO idea how they talked a ladybug into staying on that paper!).

I thought about those items for a while and then I sat by the Fairy Garden. I asked them if their names are based on trees, birds, flowers, fruits and insects. I felt this very strange buzzing sound, but I knew I had to wait for their note. I REALLY wish Fairies could talk!

The next morning the note read, "Yes, Yes, Yes!"

Okay. We were getting somewhere. But how would I ever know which Fairy had which name?

I came up with another idea. I told the Fairies that I would write some names of trees, birds, flowers, fruits and insects on separate pieces of white papers and I would tape each piece to the deck. I asked the Fairies that, if one of the papers had their name on it (in English, not Fairy), would they please stand on it and wait for me to wake up in the morning so I could see if any names were right?

I wasn't at all sure they understood what I had asked them to do but, the next morning, six Fairies were standing on the pieces of paper! I was SO excited! The Fairies and I were really beginning to understand each other. I took a picture of each of them standing on their name so I wouldn't get them mixed up (remember, there were a LOT of Fairies). That night, I thought of more names, wrote them on the paper, and waited for the morning. Seven more Fairies were waiting on the papers! I took their pictures and we did this for two straight weeks. It was actually a great deal of fun, but I was really running out of name ideas at the end!

After two weeks, every Fairy had been named and photographed. The Fairy names are as follow:

Thunder, Lightening, Storm, Dolphin, August, Robin, Blue Bird, Finch, Cardinal, Swift, Spring, Summer, Fall, Winter, Owl, Dove, Sandpiper, Daisy, Peony, Rainbow, Violet, Misty, Hummingbird,

Swan, Dawn, Sparrow, Pansy, Buttercup, Rosy, Ivy, Primrose, Lily, Larkspur, Melia, Acorn, Joy, Lemon, Lime, Daffodil, Honeysuckle, Silver Bell, Willow, Holly, Cinnamon, Spice, Breezy, Windy, Berry, Bella, Sunflower, Sweet Pea, Lark, Skye, Blue Bell, Ladybug, Gopher, Mouse, Gerbil, Hamster, Chipmunk, Butterfly, Peanut, Cherry, Blueberry, Strawberry, Scout, Dream, Wish, Wind, Peach, Poppy, Bunny, Fluffy, Tulip, Sunrise, Sunset, Wisp, Whisper, Twilight, Comet, Jupiter, Shooting Star, Badger, Blue Jay, Buddy, Buffy, Teal, and Scarlett.

13
NOW THEY WANT THEIR PICTURE TAKEN!

Both the Fairies and I were dancing with joy that we were now able to call each other by name but then, they had another request. They wanted all my grandchildren, especially Isabella, to know their names. I had been taking pictures of them standing on their name papers so I could remember their names, but I decided I would need new pictures.

I wrote three or four of their names on a piece of paper and they would each stand there in the morning so I could take 'group' pictures. They were SO cute! I had all these pieces of papers on the deck and, when I woke up in the morning, they were all standing, as still as always, on their name.

I decided I wanted to make Isabella an album with all the Fairies and their names so I thought a group shot would be a good idea. It was a BAD idea and almost a disaster. Isabella and I had noticed for years that some of the Fairies seemed to move and wiggle just a tiny bit during the day. They didn't move much but Isabella and I were VERY aware of everything that went on in the Fairy Village.

I created a nice space on the deck for a group shot and asked the Fairies to please be there in the morning so I could take their picture. I woke up the next day, made a cup of tea and wandered out to my deck. To my total shock, all the Fairies were sitting or standing patiently all together right where I had asked them to wait!

I grabbed my phone immediately and started to take the pictures. I was looking at my results and, for some reason, a great number of the boy fairies were blurred as if they had been moving. I thought I had just taken a bunch of bad pictures, so I tried again. Same results. Actually, I noticed Thunder and Lightening were not even in the second batch.

Those two boy Fairies always seemed to be causing mischief! Isabella already mentioned their names and she'll write some more about them later but, right now, I was just trying to get a group picture accomplished. I wasn't discouraged, though. I had the same problem trying to get all my HUMAN children and grandchildren to settle down for a group picture!

I used my stern 'Grandmommy' voice and said "Thunder and Lightening, get back into the group NOW. All Fairy boys, either you stop wiggling or we are going to be here all day until I get a good picture."

It worked. All the Fairy boys settled down. I do think I saw a suggestion of a smile on all the girl Fairies' faces because I had to use my "Grandmommy' voice on the boy Fairies. I guess there isn't much of a difference between Fairies and human children after all!

14
FAIRIES AND FAIRY FRIENDS

All the fairies are unique in their own way. Fairies come in different sizes, genders, and shapes. Some of the fairies are girls and some of them are boys. Some always seem to like to sit together and some seem to like to stand.

I think a lot of the reason why people think that fairies aren't real is because you can buy them on the internet as statues. We do buy the fairy statues on the internet and, once we get them, we put them in the garden. Then, the fairies in our garden tell either their friends or family members who don't have a home that there are new statues in the garden. Once the fairies enter the statues, the statue is now their daily resting place and it becomes a part of the magical world.

We also have dogs, dragons, crabs, ducks, bunnies, frogs, and sheep in our Fairy Garden. It's a little different with the animals. We do buy the animal statues also but they must be touched by a fairy to become magical creatures just like the fairies. The fairies never had pets before so they were really excited when we started adding animal statues to the Garden.

Our Fairy Garden isn't just filled with regular and ordinary fairies, it's filled with extraordinary, little, bright light miracles.

Isabella did a good job explaining that the Fairies live in their statues during the day. I have watched the Fairies for many, many, many nights and I have noticed that some of our Fairies like to have the same statue so we call them twins. We actually have a few triplets also! It took me a few years to understand why some fairies wanted the same statue as another fairy but, I finally figured it out. I liked to watch the Fairies leave their statues at night to play and I noticed that, sometimes, two or three fairies would come out of the same statue. One day, Isabella and I picked a duplicate fairy statue to buy and we put it in the garden. The next night, one of the Fairies sharing the same statue moved to the new duplicate Fairy statue! I think those Fairies are real twins or triplets and they were trying to tell me that for a long time.

15
FAIRY PERSONALITIES

I have spent seven years sitting and watching our Fairies. Plus, I have been reading their notes for most of those years (when I was little, I couldn't read!). The notes would always have funny stories or funny questions and I've learned that all fairies are different in their own ways!

Some fairies like to wear bright colors and some like the opposite. Some fairies like to be with their fairy friends; some like to find a story in a great book! There are as many similarities and differences between the fairies as there are with human children.

Because of the notes, I've learned about the personalities of so many of the fairies. I could write about every one of them but then, this book would be a hundred pages bigger! Maybe I'll write a second book about all the fairies' personalities after I finish this one. For now, here are a few of my favorite fairies.

Storm is a triplet with the garden's crazy boys (Thunder and Lightning). He is completely different than his brothers because he doesn't like to make noise or cause trouble like they do. He's quiet and he likes to hang around everyone but mostly the girls since they are calm and peaceful.

Sunrise and Sunset are girl fairies that are conjoined which means they are together forever not by choice. I like these fairies because whenever I look at them, there's no sign of disagreements or fighting. They seem to be happy being together all the time. I think I would have a hard time being with the same person all the time!

Also, there are some fairies that play musical instruments! At first, there were no boy fairies that liked to play but now two boys have joined the Fairy band. The instruments are the flute, guitar, tambourine, viola and harp. I personally can't hear the music since like, we mentioned earlier, fairies play at night. I bet their music is magical, soft and beautiful, though!

The final fairy I'd like to introduce you to is Dolphin. He is a boy fairy who loves to fish. He sits with his dog all the time and his dog seems to love being with him. I think Dolphin is an extraordinary fairy because he doesn't get into trouble and he seems to be a friend to everyone.

Our fairies may like the same statue to live in during the day but their personalities all make them unique!

16
SHAY'S WEDDING

Shay is our family friend who is the BEST friend EVER! When she asked to have her wedding at our Lake House, my Grandparents said, "Absolutely!" Of course, this didn't mean that the fairies knew what a wedding was or what it entailed. So, you better believe that we had some EXPLAINING to DO!

The first thing that we did was go online and buy the fairies some fairy size decorations for their own celebration. My Grandmommy and I bought a little miniature wedding cake, mini banners and more.

Next, we had to explain to the fairies why we were celebrating a wedding. We told them that a wedding is a celebration that joins two people together who love and care for each other. When they join together, their families also join together to make one big family. They understood that right away!

We told them that there will be little kids at the wedding that were going to want to look at the fairies and the garden. I was a little kid myself once and I knew that the little kids would be more interested in the fairies than the wedding. I didn't want the fairies to be afraid of all the attention they were going to get since the wedding was going to be performed right in FRONT of their Garden.

The day of the wedding came and I had to get myself ready since I was a Junior Bridesmaid! I couldn't wait! I had been a flower girl before but not a Junior Bridesmaid. The wedding took place in the front yard in front of the Fairy Garden (as I mentioned earlier) and the fairies were so excited. They were able to watch the whole ceremony and I was glad that I had already explained the reason for the ceremony to them.

After we did pictures and all the wedding stuff, the little girls visited the Garden and adored it! I just had to remind them not to touch the fairies. The girls followed the rule PERFECTLY and the fairies loved the attention!

Oh, did I mention that Shay is the artist of this book? Yep, she drew all the pictures that you see on these pages.

17
WHY FAIRIES PLAY AT NIGHT

Earlier in this book, I told you that Fairies only play at night. During the day, they stand or sit in their Village and try to stay very still. Since I didn't know ANYTHING about Fairies, it took me years to wonder why they couldn't play during the day. They were always very curious about US but we were also very curious about THEM.

One day while I was visiting the Fairies, I asked them to explain to me why they didn't play during the day. The next morning, I received a note placed under the note stone. You will notice their English improved every summer!

"Grandmommy, we cannot play during the day because we are very little. Whenever we would try to play fairy catch, or dare the water, or wing fast, birds would try to catch us. Squirrels would chase us, chipmunks would run after us, mice thought we were pieces of cheese. We are much faster so they never caught us but it is not fun to play if you always have to be watching for danger."

I simply never had thought of that! I certainly wouldn't want to be smaller than a mouse! I was interested, though, in the games the Fairies had written about to me. I asked them, after I read the note, to explain their games to me and I asked if their games were similar to human children games. They responded, as always, the next morning.

"Grandmommy, we have some games we have played for many, many summers but we love watching your human children play their games. Every night, we try to play the same games and we have so much fun!"

I was really enjoying this conversation with the Fairies! I was learning about what their life was like and it fascinated me. I asked them to explain the fairy games to me because I didn't know how to play 'fairy catch', 'dare the water', or 'wing fast'.

They replied, "Grandmommy, we think we are 'teacher' just like Isabella! We teach you now. 'Fairy catch' is when one fairy tries to catch other fairy and then that fairy tries to do the catching. We don't like to get our wings wet because it is harder to fly with wet wings but the boys like to play 'dare the water'. They fly as close to the Lake waves without getting wet. Lightening always gets so wet that the other boys must help him back to the Village because he can't fly. We don't know how human children can play in the waves! 'Wing fast' is all fairies flying as fast as we can and see which fairy flies over Garden first."

When I read that note, I laughed and said that we call 'Fairy catch' by the name of 'Tag" and 'Wing fast' is a race. Human children really don't play 'dare the water' because they call it swimming and they don't have wings to get wet.

The Fairies responded the next day. "Sometimes, we forget human children not fairies!"

18
FAIRIES CAN TALK!

For some reason, Fairies always answered our questions in writing. We could talk to them and we know they could understand us because they always answered in a note the next day. I always thought it would be so much easier if they learned to speak English but that would be asking too much of them. We were all grateful that, somehow, they could understand us and write back to us in English. That was magic enough!

One day, I was cleaning up the Fairy Garden (it's under two big trees so I'm always cleaning up acorns, leaves, and twigs) and I kept hearing this humming sound. To be honest, I thought it was a mosquito and I dislike mosquitoes a lot, so I kept swatting around my head. Suddenly, the humming started sounding like 'Grandmommy, Grandmommy, Grandmommy'. I stopped cleaning and sat very still. Then I said, "Are you saying my name?" The humming started again but I was listening VERY closely and I could hear "Yes, Yes,

Yes! Grandmommy, Grandmommy, Grandmommy!"

The Fairies HAD been talking to us all the time but the world is so noisy, we never heard them! Their voices, even all together, sound like the faintest of whispers, like the sigh of the wind.

19
THE FAIRIES' FAREWELL

One night, I was sitting on the deck with my friends Denise and Judy. It was very late and we were just relaxing before going to bed. It was in September, and the Lake House was going to be closed for the winter, so we were enjoying the last night listening to the waves roll over the beach and watching the sun disappear behind the trees.

I have always liked to look at my Fairy Garden and when I looked over at it that night, I saw a light. I smiled because I knew my friends had never seen the Fairies playing and they were in for a real treat.

I whispered to my friends, "The Fairies are coming out to play." They turned to look and, suddenly, about fifty Fairies were all out of their statues and just hovering over the Garden. I had never seen them do that. Not ever. Usually, when they come out to play, they fly out in small groups and start playing high in the trees. I've never seen them all be ready to play at the same time.

I leaned forward in my chair and looked closely at the Fairies. Then, I got up and started walking towards them. I said to Denise and Judy, "Be very quiet. I think they want to talk to us."

As I approached the Fairy Village, the night was still and quiet. I stopped around three feet from all the Fairies hovering in the air and I said, "Fairies, do you want to talk to me?" I listened as hard as I could but I couldn't hear anything. Then a very sad idea came into my head. I said, "Fairies, are you trying to say goodbye for the summer?"

All the Fairies bobbed up and down at the same time and I heard, "Yes, Grandmommy, it is time for us to leave."

At first, I was excited because I had actually HEARD them but then I realized that, again, they were leaving.

I said, "Oh, it's so hard for me to say goodbye to you, but it would be easier if I can hear you promise that you'll come back next year."

They all started to laugh! I could hear their laughter, and even my friends heard it!
It sounded like bells or chimes ringing in the wind. The Fairies said, "Of course, we will come back next summer! WE LOVE YOU AND YOUR SPECIAL LITTLE HUMANS!" All fifty bright, little lights (the Fairies) danced for a minute in front of me and then, flew into the sky. They were gone.

Well, of course, I started to cry both tears of happiness and tears of sadness because I was sad to see them leave. I walked over to my friends and then, I was happy again! One of my friends had recorded the whole event on her phone. Not only could I watch it over and over when I missed the Fairies but I could show the video to my Grandchildren! I couldn't wait to show it to Isabella!

When I first saw the video of the fairies flying away for the Winter, I was amazed! First, the fairies had a conversation with my Grandmommy! I've never heard the fairies talk to me. It doesn't mean that they haven't tried to do so but maybe I wasn't listening hard enough. Anyway, when I watched the video, my first reaction was, "NNOOOOOOO, they left the Fairy Garden!" I felt really, really sad for a moment because I always enjoy having them as friends while I'm up at the Lake. Then, my brother watched the video and his eyes got bigger and bigger. Right after we finished watching it, I looked at my brother and said, "I told you so." I told him this because he was starting to not believe in fairies anymore. The video is proof that fairies DO exist!

I felt happy for our fairies, though, because I didn't want them to turn into little ice cubes over the Winter. Overall, I don't know what the Lake House would feel like if the fairies weren't part of it. The fairies have always been Family to us from the day they decided to make our Lake House their summer home!

ALWAYS BELIEVE

Fairies are all around us. You do not need a special Fairy Garden or a Lake House. You just need to BELIEVE in magic. If you can do that, look around and you will see a light in the sky, you might hear the softest of whispers, or feel a tickle on the back on your neck. Smile and say, "I know you're there, little Fairy, and I want to be your friend!"